Tag!

First published in 2008 by
Franklin Watts
338 Euston Road
London
NW1 3BH

Franklin Watts Australia
Level 17/207 Kent Street
Sydney
NSW 2000

A CIP catalogue record for this book is available
from the British Library.

ISBN 978 0 7496 7969 9 (hbk)
ISBN 978 0 7496 7975 0 (pbk)

Series Editor: Jackie Hamley
Editor: Melanie Palmer
Series Advisor: Dr Hilary Minns
Series Designer: Peter Scoulding

Printed in China

Franklin Watts is a division of
Hachette Children's Books,
an Hachette Livre UK company.

For Juliette with love
and all best wishes - A.B.

Tag!

by Ann Bryant

Illustrated by Kirsteen H. Jones

W

FRANKLIN WATTS

LONDON•SYDNEY

Ann Bryant
"I've only got
a cat for a pet,
but I think a pig
might be quite nice,
especially one like
Sid the Pig who
would do the
cooking for me!"

JS

**Kirsteen H.
Jones**
"Creating the
characters for this
re-telling of the three
little pigs story was lots of
fun, especially the wolf
with his hungry
expression!"

Sid the pig was cooking when ...

...Wolf came to
the door.

7

Sid ran to Dan's house.

Wolf chased him.

"Quick! Run!" said Sid.
"Wolf is coming!"

"Ha, ha!" laughed Wolf.

Sid and Dan
ran and ran ...

... to Mick's house.

But Mick forgot to lock the door.

17

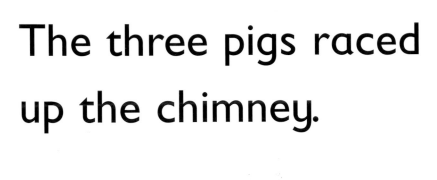

The three pigs raced
up the chimney.

19

But they didn't get far.

"Tag!" said Wolf.
"Now you're IT!"

23

Notes for adults

TADPOLES are structured to provide support for newly independent readers. The stories may also be used by adults for sharing with young children.

Starting to read alone can be daunting. **TADPOLES** help by providing visual support and repeating words and phrases. These books will both develop confidence and encourage reading and rereading for pleasure.

If you are reading this book with a child, here are a few suggestions:

1. Make reading fun! Choose a time to read when you and the child are relaxed and have time to share the story.
2. Talk about the story before you start reading. Look at the cover and the blurb. What might the story be about? Why might the child like it?
3. Encourage the child to reread the story, and to retell the story in their own words, using the illustrations to remind them what has happened.
4. Discuss the story and see if the child can relate it to their own experience, or perhaps compare it to another story they know.
5. Give praise! Remember that small mistakes need not always be corrected.

If you enjoyed this book, why not try another TADPOLES story?

* hardback